Red Red
Red

Red

Red

Valeri Gorbachev

PHILOMEL BOOKS

One summer evening Turtle is rushing through town.

"Where are you going in such a hurry, Turtle?"
asks Mrs. Raccoon.

"I am off to see something red, red, red," says
Turtle without stopping.

"Something red?" Mrs. Raccoon says. "Is it my red roses?"

"No, no, no," says Turtle. "It's not your red roses."

"Then what is it?" asks Mrs. Raccoon, following
Turtle right past Rabbit's Grocery Store.
But Turtle doesn't answer.

"Where are you going in such a hurry, friends?"
asks Rabbit.

"Turtle is off to see something red," says Mrs.
Raccoon. "But he is in such a hurry he has no time
to tell me what it is! I am going to see for myself."

"Maybe it is my red tomatoes, or my red cherries,
or even my red watermelon," says Rabbit.
"No, no, no. It is not your tomatoes or cherries or
watermelon," Turtle says, hurrying on.

"But what is it then?" says Rabbit, getting in line behind Mrs. Raccoon and Turtle and passing neighbor Goat, who is collecting his laundry.

But Turtle doesn't answer.

So Goat calls out, "Where are you going in such a hurry, neighbors?"

"We don't know," says Rabbit. "Turtle is off to see something red, but he is in such a hurry he has no time to tell us what it is."

"Can it be my red socks?" asks neighbor Goat.
"No, no, no," says Turtle, without missing a
step. "It is not your red socks."

"But what is it?" begs neighbor Goat as he falls in line behind Rabbit, Mrs. Raccoon and Turtle just as they are passing neighbor Fox's house, where she is painting the roof.

Turtle doesn't answer.

Then Fox calls out, "Where are you going in such a hurry, neighbors?"

"We just don't know," says Goat. "Turtle is off to see something red, but he is in such a hurry he has no time to tell us what it is."

"Maybe it is the roof of my house!" says Fox. "I am painting it red!"

"No, no, no," says Turtle. "It is not your red roof." And he hurries on.

"Then what is it?" asks Fox as she falls in line behind Goat, Rabbit, Mrs. Raccoon and Turtle. She is curious, too.

They all pass the firehouse.

"What's going on here?" cries a firefighter. "Where are you going in such a hurry?"

"We don't know. We are all following Turtle," says Fox. "He is off to see something red, and he is in such a hurry he has no time to tell us what it is."

The firefighters grow alarmed. Something red? And they fall in line behind Fox, Goat, Rabbit, Mrs. Raccoon and Turtle, just as they all come to the lake and see Captain Dog and his ship next to the pier.

"Where are you going in such a hurry?" Captain Dog cries from his ship. "We don't know. Turtle is off to see something red, and he has no time to tell us what it is!"

"It must be my ship," says Captain Dog.
"Its bottom is red and it has a red smokestack
and red life preservers."

"No, no, no," says Turtle. "It's not your
ship." And he hurries on.

"Then what is it?" the surprised Captain Dog
says as he falls in line behind the firefighters,
Fox, Goat, Rabbit, Mrs. Raccoon and Turtle.
"I would like to know."

But Turtle doesn't answer him.

They all climb up the hill to the lake.

"Here we are," says Turtle, taking a deep breath at the top of the hill.

"Where is red, red, red?" cries a firefighter. "I see nothing red here."

Goat, Fox, Rabbit, and Mrs. Raccoon join him. "Why were we in such a rush, Turtle?"

"Look over there," whispers Turtle. "The red, red, red . . . is coming!"

"AHHHHHHHH," they all sigh happily together.
"It's the sunset."
    "Yes, it's the beautiful red sunset," says Turtle,
and all of them turn to enjoy it . . .

. . . and all of them stay until the big
yellow moon appears in the evening sky.
"Perfect," Turtle takes the time to say.

For Esther   —V G

Patricia Lee Gauch, editor

PHILOMEL BOOKS
A division of Penguin Young Readers Group.
Published by The Penguin Group. Penguin Group (USA) Inc., 375 Hudson Street, New York, NY 10014, U.S.A.
Penguin Group (Canada), 90 Eglinton Avenue East, Suite 700, Toronto, Ontario, Canada M4P 2Y3 (a division of Pearson Penguin Canada Inc.).
Penguin Books Ltd, 80 Strand, London WC2R 0RL, England.
Penguin Ireland, 25 St. Stephen's Green, Dublin 2, Ireland (a division of Penguin Books Ltd.).
Penguin Group (Australia), 250 Camberwell Road, Camberwell, Victoria 3124, Australia (a division of Pearson Australia Group Pty Ltd).
Penguin Books India Pvt Ltd, 11 Community Centre, Panchsheel Park, New Delhi - 110 017, India.
Penguin Group (NZ), Cnr Airborne and Rosedale Roads, Albany, Auckland 1310, New Zealand (a division of Pearson New Zealand Ltd).
Penguin Books (South Africa) (Pty) Ltd, 24 Sturdee Avenue, Rosebank, Johannesburg 2196, South Africa.
Penguin Books Ltd, Registered Offices: 80 Strand, London WC2R 0RL, England.

Design by Semadar Megged. The text is set in 17-point Horley Old Style. The illustrations are rendered in pen-and-ink and watercolors.

Library of Congress Cataloging-in-Publication Data Gorbachev, Valeri. Red red red / Valeri Gorbachev. p. cm. Summary: As Turtle rushes through town, in a hurry to see something "red, red, red," his neighbors wonder what it could be and hurry after him to find out. [1. Turtles—Fiction. 2. Red—Fiction. 3. Curiosity—Fiction. 4. Animals—Fiction.] I. Title. PZ7.G6475Red 2007 [E]—dc22 2006014265 ISBN 978-0-399-24628-9
Special Markets ISBN 978-0-399-25208-2 Not for Resale